Ladybugs

of Wisteria Hollow

by

Winifred Reed and Avony Green

Contents

Ladybugs of Wisteria Hollow
by Winifred Reed and Avony Green

Published in the United States of America ISBN: 978-1-62510-755-8

KDP ISBN 9798560740559

1. Juvenile Fiction /Educational/Magical/Inspiring
2. Juvenile Fiction /Imagination & Fantasy

This book is dedicated to you, the reader. I believe if we all took the opportunity to get to know and appreciate others who look different from us, we would meet very interesting people, make new friends, and make the world a better place.

Acknowledgments

To Branford Dodd, Evelyn Finley and Ardith Provo,
thank you for your support in the initial editing.
To my children (Stephanie, Gary and Thamarian),
thank you for your support, love,
and encouragement.

Avony and her parents lived in a lovely two-story house.

The tall trees that lined the streets of the neighborhood created a picturesque view.

Avony loved to draw and paint very colorful pictures, and because she loved colors so much, Avony and her parents decided to plant colorful flowers in the front yard.

They spent hours working and planting different flowers and bushes in the yard to create a beautiful scene.

By the beginning of summer, the front yard was a dazzling display of the yellow and white lilies, pink roses, cone-shaped pine trees, and large, green elephant ears.

There were also red cannas, yellow gladiolas, blue hydrangeas, and butterfly bushes covered in green leaves with orange flowers.

In the middle of the yard was an old wisteria bush that was planted years before Avony and her parents purchased the house. It was covered with very large purple clusters of flowers that almost touched the ground because the bush was growing crooked from being in many windstorms.

The previous owners tried to train the bush to grow straight but it was so crooked that nothing worked.

The base of the wisteria was very thick because it was so old. Avony loved the big purple clusters of flowers that hung from the bush, but her mother wanted to replace the bush since it was so warped. Avony's mother assured her that they would plant another wisteria bush that would grow straight and tall.

One day Avony's mother decided it was time to cut down the wisteria bush. She took an axe from the garage and walked up to the bush. Expecting to cut it down with one swing, she hit the bush, but the axe only vibrated the bush. After several attempts, she realized she had barely dented it. Feeling tired, Avony's mother thought, "*This is really a strong bush, but it needs to go"!* Then she asked her husband to get the chainsaw and cut the wisteria down.

He placed the chainsaw up against the bush, but it was slow to penetrate through the tough old bark. He did not quit, and finally the bush fell over. Avony's parents were too tired to dig up the stump and decided they would dig it up later.

Avony stood in her bedroom window and watched her parents cut down the bush. She knew she would miss seeing the purple clusters of flowers, but she understood why her mother wanted to cut the wisteria down.

Days went by, and Avony's parents had not dug up the stump. One day Avony walked up to it and closed her eyes. She made a wish that the bush would grow again and be straight so her mother would like it.

Two weeks later Avony was outside playing. She looked down and noticed two tiny red-and-black ladybugs that were identical to each other. She got on her knees and followed the ladybugs right up to the wisteria stump.

"What are you looking at, Avony?" asked her mother.

"Two ladybugs by this wisteria stump," Avony responded. Knowing that Avony liked insects, her mother said, "Don't bring them in the house."

Avony responded, "I won't, besides, they crawled into a hole in the stump, and I can't see them now."

Avony's mother said, "Well, they had better come out before we dig up that old stump."

Avony became concerned about the ladybugs and thought she needed to figure out another home for them before her parents dug the stump up leaving the ladybugs homeless.

Avony ran upstairs to her room and found a box. She rushed back to the stump and placed the box as close to the hole as she could, propping the lid partially open. She hoped the two bugs would crawl inside.

Avony could not wait until the next morning to see if the ladybugs crawled into the box. She hoped they liked the box more than the stump so it could be their temporary home while she looked for another bush for them to live.

The next morning, Avony hurried downstairs to check the box. When she opened it, she was surprised to see it was filled with ladybugs!

Her eyes opened wide as she noticed the bugs were all different. Avony had only seen red-and-black ladybugs before. She had no idea that ladybugs came in so many different colors, shapes, and sizes. She noticed that the two little red-and-black ladybugs were not in the box.

She was excited about seeing different types and colors of ladybugs, but she was very concerned about the two red-and-black ladybugs.

There were ladybugs with white spots and black spots. Some of the ladybugs had up to twenty spots, and some had no spots at all. Some were round and fat, and others were oblong and skinny. The ladybugs were pink, black, red, orange, yellow, and brown.

Looking at the ladybugs was like watching a fashion show because of their many colors, shapes, sizes, and spots. The one Avony was most surprised to see was the ladybug with stripes.

She admired the bugs and set the box back on the ground hoping the two bugs would crawl inside later that day.

Avony was so excited about discovering the different types of ladybugs that she wanted to tell her parents.

She ran back into the house and asked her parents to come look at the ladybugs.

When Avony's parents looked at the ladybugs, they were surprised too and told Avony they would do more research about ladybugs on the Internet.

The family went back into the house and turned on the computer. Avony's father typed the word *ladybugs* so he could help Avony answer her questions about ladybugs. Avony read that a group of ladybugs is called a loveliness. Avony said, "I like that they are called loveliness because they really are lovely little bugs."

Avony's mom agreed and said, "Well, I hope the loveliness of ladybugs is not harmful to our lovely flowers."

Avony and her parents kept reading and found out that some of the names for ladybugs were convergent, black ladybug, seven-spotted ladybug, and pink-spotted ladybug and that they came from different parts of the world.

They read that ladybugs were part of the beetle family and that there were over five thousand species.

They were happy to read that some ladybugs were known for protecting plants from other insects. Avony and her parents liked the fact that these were good bugs and they would not harm the flowers and other plants in the yard.

Avony asked, "Did you know the ladybugs have two sets of wings?"

They searched for information about the anatomy of ladybugs and found that they did have two sets of wings. The colorful hard cover on the back of ladybugs is a wing called the elytra.

"The two wings on the outside are identical, and they protect the more delicate wings underneath," explained Avony's mom.

Avony and her mom read more about ladybugs and found out that ladybugs came from six of the seven continents. They come from Europe, Asia, North America, South America, Australia, and Africa.

Avony thought about all the different ladybugs she had collected and wondered if there were still other colors of bugs inside the stump.

Avony wanted to observe how all the ladybugs lived together, so she had to find a way to see inside the stump.

The next day she took her magnifying glass and placed the glass lens over a small hole of the stump. Avony could not believe what she saw!

There were many other colors of ladybugs and they were moving back and forth like a busy colony of ants. She also noticed that the ladybugs huddled together by their color. Avony wondered why the bugs didn't mingle with each other instead of staying segregated if they all lived in one space.

Avony picked up a tiny stick and forced two bugs beside each other to see what would happen. As soon as she moved the stick, the two bugs rushed away from each other. She remembered that even in the box the bugs moved to sections to avoid touching each other.

Avony thought, *"These ladybugs don't like each other".* She knew she could not do anything about that, so she went inside knowing she would check on the bugs the next day.

Avony arose early so she could go out and check on the ladybugs.

When Avony walked outside, she heard a tapping sound in a nearby tree.

She searched and searched until she spotted the most unusual bird. The bird had a small tip of feathers on his head. It appeared to be wearing a mask over his face. His body was long and skinny, and he had long tail feathers.

Avony went back inside the house and told her mother about the bird pecking the tree really hard and fast.

As soon as Avony said the bird was pecking really fast in the same spot, her mother knew it was a woodpecker.

Avony's mother said, "Let's look in your bird book and see if we can find a picture of the bird."

As soon as Avony's mother turned to the page with a woodpecker, Avony yelled, "That is the one! That is the bird!"

Avony thought the woodpecker was beautiful, but she was still very concerned about the ladybugs. Avony wondered if the woodpecker would eventually start pecking on the stump where the ladybugs lived.

She worried about the woodpecker eating the ladybugs if they crawled out of the stump. Avony did not like the woodpecker being so close to the ladybugs' home.

While she was upstairs, Avony looked out her window and noticed a woodpecker on the fence just feet away from the stump, and she knew the bird had probably spotted the bugs. She ran downstairs and rushed out the door.

She shushed the woodpecker away, but as soon as she walked back inside, the woodpecker returned to the fence. Avony knew the woodpecker was determined to make it to the stump to eat the ladybugs.

She had to do something to protect the bugs, so she picked up a rock and threw it at the bird. The bird flew away again, but Avony knew it was only temporary. Avony watched the stump and the woodpecker all day.

She knew she would have to give up on making the bird fly away because it was getting late. Avony thought about putting a cover over the stump but thought the ladybugs would not like it.

Her mother explained that it was not Avony's duty to protect the ladybugs and they would be fine.

It was almost bedtime for Avony, and she was tired. She hoped the woodpecker would not return that night. She hoped the ladybugs would stay inside the stump, but she knew they would come out eventually. As she climbed into bed, Avony heard the woodpecker pecking on a tree.

She thought that if the woodpecker was pecking on the tree, she would know that the bugs were safe. She also hoped that the woodpecker would peck all night and be too tired to bother the ladybugs at daybreak. She tried to stay awake and listen to the woodpecker, but she soon fell asleep.

Early the next morning, Avony woke up and looked out the window to see the sun shining bright. She looked down at the stump and saw the woodpecker on the wisteria stump.

Avony rushed downstairs, out the door, and toward the stump, yelling, “Get away! Shoo!”

The bird flew away, but as soon as Avony turned around to go back into the house, the woodpecker flew back to the stump. Avony thought, *I have got to do something, or that bird is going to eat all the ladybugs!*

Avony stood helplessly in the doorway and watched the woodpecker on the stump; then she saw the woodpecker peck at the ground.

She knew the bird had picked up a ladybug in its beak. She felt sad because she thought it might be one of the red-and-black ladybugs. Suddenly, the bird dropped the ladybug and flew away. Avony thought the bird seemed angry. She wondered if it would come back.

Avony's mother walked to the door and asked, "Avony, what are you looking at?"

"That woodpecker picked up one of the ladybugs in its beak but then dropped it!"

Avony's mother replied, "Yes, ladybugs are tiny, but I read that they secrete a powerful toxin that most predators dislike." Come eat, Avony, I do not think you need to worry about the ladybugs being eaten by that bird. Ladybugs are small, but they pack a powerful defense."

Avony was happy about the toxin that the ladybugs had in their bodies to protect them from predators. Later that day, Avony went to the stump with her magnifying glass again and laid it on the hole. Then she went back into the house to get her camera. She was so tired from running up and down the stairs to check on the ladybugs that she decided to sit on her bed and rest for a few minutes; then she laid back on her bed planning to just rest for a minute, but instead of resting for a minute, she fell asleep.

She walked outside and saw a yellow glow shining from the hole of the stump. She realized she left the magnifying glass on the stump and thought she may have made it too hot for the ladybugs, and that she may have caused all the ladybugs to die.

She rushed to the stump and pressed her eye close to the magnifying glass. Suddenly, something magical happened. A bright light shined in Avony's eyes, and she fell back from the stump.

She decided to take another look, and not only could she see the ladybugs more clearly, she could hear them! She could not believe that she could hear them talking.

She knew it was magic, and she did not know if she should tell her parents. She thought they would never believe her. She did not believe it herself.

Avon decided to just listen to the bugs for a while. She realized that the woodpecker was not the only problem.

The bugs were arguing over which bugs had rights to stay in the hollow stump and which ones had to move.

The European ladybugs lived in the bottom of the stump, and the other bugs lived higher at different levels of the bush before Avon's mother cut the bush down.

All the bugs fell to the bottom level of the bush from the vibrations of the axe and chainsaw.

They were willing to put up with each other for a little while, but they thought the stump would soon be too small for all the different species. Having to share the same spot left the bugs tired, frustrated, and angry with each other.

Avony did not know what they were going to do if they could not work out the problem of different species in one space.

Avony put her mouth near the hole and said, "Hello! Hello! Hello, little bugs. I can hear you, and you all really need to try to get along."

One ladybug looked up at Avony and screamed, "Monster! Monster!" All the bugs were trying to figure out what was wrong with the screaming bug. Then it screamed, "Look up!"

All the bugs looked up and saw Avony and scrambled in a panic for safety, but there was nowhere to take cover except behind each other.

Avony said, "Don't panic. I won't hurt you."

One baby bug yelled, "Who are you, and what do you want?"

Avony responded, "I want to help you all find a better home because my parents are going to dig up this old stump. None of you will be able to stay here, so stop fighting among yourselves and work together."

"Why do you want to help us?" asked the pink bug.

"Well," said Avony, "I have been doing research about ladybugs, and I did not know you came in so many different shapes, sizes, colors, and spots. I like ladybugs, but I thought you only came in red with black spots."

Avony continued, saying, "I know that you are part of the beetle family and that some of you are good for gardens and crops, and most birds don't like the taste of ladybugs."

She continued, saying, "You also have another problem."

"What!" shouted one of the red ladybug leaders.

Avony said, "There is a woodpecker that might want to peck on this stump, and now he is angry because he does not like the taste of ladybugs! He may come back to attack you!"

Avony noticed that the baby bugs played well together and wished that the older bugs could get along too.

She saw the same two identical bugs she saw earlier and yelled, "What are your names?"

The two bugs quickly crawled closer to Avony, and one of them replied in a high-pitched voice, "Hi, my name is Tickle, and this is my twin brother Tackle."

Avony giggled at the name of the two bugs. Her giggle caused the other bugs to calm down as they realized Avony was not out to hurt them. They also thought she could be trusted a little since she knew so much about ladybugs.

Avony said, "So you are male ladybugs."

An old, striped ladybug spoke up and said, "Yes, we are all called ladybugs, but there are male and female ladybugs." Avony remembered reading on the Internet that the name ladybug came from European farmers praying to the Virgin Mary to save their crops, and in other countries, ladybugs were considered good luck.

According to Avony's research, ladybugs did protect the crops, and they were called lady beetles; then later they were called ladybugs regardless of whether they were male or female."

Avony warned the bugs, saying, "This hollow base is large enough for all of you right now, and you all need to stay inside from the mean, woodpecker.

A brown ladybug said,"But we don't like yellow ladybugs."

A red ladybug said, "And we don't like brown ladybugs."

"Well, what about white or pink ladybugs?" asked Avony.

The yellow, brown, and red bugs responded, "Definitely don't like them."

Avony knew the bugs had a problem that needed to be resolved and quickly.

One bug that had no spots said, "I don't know why we don't like each other. I just know that we are not supposed to like any bug that looks different."

Avony responded loudly, "You are all ladybugs. That is nonsense. Have you tried talking and getting to know each other?"

"Well no, there is nothing to talk about. We are superior to all the other ladybugs, and they need to be separate from us," replied the brown bug.

“The pink bugs have a strange accent, and the yellow ones can speak a totally different language,” said the orange ladybug.

“Then there are the fat bugs that always seem too happy, and the skinny yellow ones are always too loud,” interrupted the yellow ladybug.

“One other thing, the orange ones never seem to sleep!” yelled a pink bug. “We are just too different to live together.” An orange ladybug yelled,“The pink bugs are just boring!” Avony said, “But you all are ladybugs. You have different strengths, and if you pull together, you would be a stronger

group to fight off the woodpecker.”

She continued, “The orange bugs can post guard while the others rest.”Then she said, “The loud ones can send great alarms when the woodpecker is spotted. The fat bugs can carry more food for the group on their backs, and the ones that are always happy can decrease tension and improve communication among the group.”

One yellow leader ladybug yelled, “Go away! We do not need your advice. May the strongest loveliness win this spot!” “You might win this spot, but you won’t win against the woodpecker!” yelled Avony. “Why don’t you just work together and see what each group has to offer? It may not be easy since there is so much discontent between you all,

but it is worth a try.”

“What is discontent?” asked one bug.

“It means that you are angry, uncomfortable, and dislike each other. Right now each species will go to great lengths to force the other species out,” said Avony.

“Yep, there is a lot of discontentment going on in here,” said the orange ladybug.

"You should not dislike a group when you don't even know anything about it."

"Well, I guess I can try to get to know the other ones, but this won't be easy," said the pink ladybug.

"I am proud of you for stepping up to the task, Ms. Pink Ladybug," said Avony.

The ladybug looked up at Avony and smiled as she winked and nodded her head. Avony smiled and winked back.

The brown bug finally agreed to talk and get to know the other bugs. Finally, the orange and white ladybugs agreed to try to get along with each other too.

"Great, I will check on you all tomorrow," said Avony as she stood up to go back inside.

When the bugs started talking, they found out that they really did have a lot in common.

In the meantime, Avony felt good that she did not see or hear the woodpecker.

Then she looked out her window, and to her surprise, the woodpecker was perched on a nearby fence. Avony tapped on her window, but the woodpecker was not afraid of her and just looked at her.

After waiting for a little while, the woodpecker flew down to the stump again and started pecking the stump. All the ladybugs were huddled together in the hollow away from the opening.

The yellow and the pink leader ladybugs yelled to all the other bugs, saying, “It is time for us to come together as one and stop fighting among ourselves.”

Tickle and Tackle yelled, “Please! Please do it for the future generations. Please!”

“Join hands!” yelled the old, striped ladybug, and all the ladybugs in the hollow put their differences aside and joined hands and started chanting, “United, united, united we stand! United, united, united, we can!”

The bugs just kept repeating the chant, getting louder each time. The woodpecker pecked frantically, trying to penetrate the stump.

Suddenly, the tree trunk started changing colors, and magical dust in colors of yellow, red, pink, white, and brown flowed up out of the stump and filled the air.

When the woodpecker saw the dust, he became frightened and tried to fan it away with his wings, but the dust just kept pouring out of the stump.

The woodpecker flew to the fence post and waited for the dust to clear, and the ladybugs thought he was gone.

The ladybugs started to celebrate the defeat over the woodpecker, by dancing, clapping, and singing.

The dust finally started to clear. Suddenly, the ladybugs heard a flapping sound and realized that the woodpecker was at the base of the stump again, but he was not pecking. He was shocked at what he saw when the dust cleared.

The stump had turned to solid gold! The bugs were totally silent, waiting to see what the woodpecker was going to do to the golden stump.

Finally after many painful attempts, the woodpecker decided to give up on destroying the stump.

All the ladybugs cheered and started to celebrate again. Suddenly, the stump changed back to its original color.

Branches started to grow on the stump, and right before Avony's eyes, she witnessed a remarkable thing. Not only had the wisteria bush grown back even more beautiful than before, but instead of being a bush, it turned into a wisteria tree! It was an unbelievable sight.

The purple clusters hung flawlessly. The tree kept growing and was the most beautiful tree she had ever seen.

Avony woke up and stretched as she looked around the room. She sat up in her bed and realized that the bad experience with the ladybugs and the woodpecker was all a dream! She sighed with relief. She realized that getting to know others, getting along with others, and working together really could add strength and power to a group. She felt like she had learned a valuable lesson about how much better the world would be if people would take the time to get to know other people who seem to be different.

Avony went outside to see if she saw any signs of ladybugs. As soon as she walked up to the stump, she saw ladybugs busily going in and out of the stump. She saw different species of ladybugs working together and that the bugs no longer cared about being different. Avony knew that the bugs worked out their problems on their own and realized they could all live peacefully together. This made Avony very happy.

Avony's parents realized how important the stump was to her and decided to not dig up the stump. Her parents explained that the wisteria was starting to grow, and they would have to train it to grow straight. They took extra-special care of the wisteria, and it did grow straight.

One day Avony noticed new sprouts growing out of the stump. Avony was very happy because she knew that the wisteria bush would continue to be home for the ladybugs and a constant reminder of how important it is to get along with others.

Today, wisteria continues to grow beautifully in the middle of Avony's yard. So the next time you see a wisteria bush, look closely; you just might see a ladybug with twenty spots, or maybe even see Tickle and Tackle's relatives.

The End

www.ingramcontent.com/pod-product-compliance
Lightning Source LLC
LaVergne TN
LVHW021314160826
845679LV00001B/343

* 9 7 9 8 5 6 0 7 4 0 5 5 9 *